I SEE

THE WORLD

AROUND ME

DW LONG, LCSW

For Aunt Virginia.

Thank you for teaching me to stop and
see the world around me.

When the mornings come, I rise and shine.
The sun is bright and I'm feeling just fine.
I can feel the smile on my smiling face.
Today I'm going to my favourite place!

Another great day has happened somehow
Where life is wonderful and happy and free.
I stop to be in the here and now
To see the world around me.

When I get outside the sky is clear.
I hear the birds singing with a musical cheer.
I stop to breathe the freshness of the air,
And feel the breeze blowing through my hair.

The best day yet has arrived, it's true!
It's the best day yet, I'll guarantee!
A great day for me to discover something new,
To stop and breathe and see the world around me.

The pups are playing with their favourite toy.
Their yips and yaps are filled with joy!
Round the garden they run as fast as can be,
Running and jumping and chasing me!

It's here again! It's another day,
A day that is sweet, a day to be free,
And as my troubles fly away,
I see the world around me.

Let's go to the barn and see the chicks.
Believe it or not, I taught them some tricks.
Their names are Peggy, Cindy and Betty,
And they are performing perfectly already!

It's a super day, a day for more fun,
A beautiful day, you wouldn't disagree!
And as I stand beneath the warm sun
I stop and breathe and see the world around me.

The butterflies float on the breeze as its blowing,
And under the sun the flowers are growing.
The bees buzz by under a clear blue sky,
And now it's time to say goodbye.

Goodbye to the flowers and the bees and the sun.
See ya later to the pups and chicks who run free.
It's been a super day, a day full of fun,
And again, I stop to see the world around me.

The evening is coming, it's on its way,
And once again it's been a beautiful day!
At the end of the day when all is said and done,
I remember that all of it has been lots of fun!

So, as bedtime arrives and we get ready to rest,
I get tucked in my bed all snug like a pea.
And thankful I am since today was the best,
Grateful for pausing to see the world around me!

The

Dw Long is a Clinical Social Worker who loves everything there is to love about being in nature! Whether he is exploring the wilds of Southeast Asia, hiking in the Scottish highlands or poking around a beach anywhere in the world, his motto is "wherever there is nature, there is magic!"

Lightning Source UK Ltd.
Milton Keynes UK
UKHW051018110621
385087UK00010B/95

9 781527 295926